NICK JR.
DORA the EXPLORER®

Dora Helps Diego!

by Laura Dris[...]
illustrated by Tom [...]

D1370329

SCHOLASTIC INC.
New York Toronto London Auckland Sydney
Mexico City New Delhi Hong Kong Buenos Aires

ISBN-13: 978-0-439-92236-4
ISBN-10: 0-439-92236-4

12 11 10 9 8 7 6 5 4 3 2 1   7 8 9 10 11 12/0

Printed in the U.S.A.

First Scholastic printing, January 2007

Hi! I am .
DORA

, , and I

need your help!

Oh, no! is missing!

BABY JAGUAR

 cannot find him!

DIEGO

 and I

BOOTS

are helping find him.

DIEGO

Will you help too?

Great!

Help us find 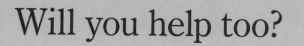BABY JAGUAR !

Look up in that  TREE .

I see a TAIL .

has a .

BABY JAGUAR   TAIL

Does it belong to ?

BABY JAGUAR

No.

It is a
SNAKE

getting out of the ☀.
SUN

Where is  ?

BABY JAGUAR

Look behind those .

FLOWERS

I see . .

FEET

has .

BABY JAGUAR   FEET

Do they belong to ?

BABY JAGUAR

No.

It is
ISA

working in her .
GARDEN

Where is  ?

BABY JAGUAR

Look behind that trunk.

TREE

I see .

WHISKERS

 BABY JAGUAR has  WHISKERS.

Do those  WHISKERS belong

to BABY JAGUAR ?

No.

It is  SWIPER, that sneaky fox.

Where is
BABY JAGUAR ?

Look behind the .
SLIDE

I see .
SPOTS

 has  .

BABY JAGUAR   SPOTS

Do they belong to  ?

BABY JAGUAR

No.

It is the scarf that

belongs to .
BENNY

Will we **ever** find  ?
BABY JAGUAR

We need to go back to

the Animal Rescue Center.

We open the .

DOOR

We cannot believe it!

We see a ,
TAIL

,
FEET

, and
WHISKERS

.
SPOTS

Here is  !
BABY JAGUAR

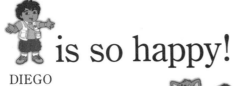 is so happy!

DIEGO

We found !

BABY JAGUAR

Thanks for helping!